Tiger

and th
Temper Tantrum

For Ruby

KINGFISHER
An imprint of Kingfisher Publications Plc
New Penderel House, 283-288 High Holborn
London WC1V 7HZ
www.kingfisherpub.com

First published in hardback by Kingfisher 1999
First published in paperback by Kingfisher 2002
2 4 6 8 10 9 7 5 3 1
1TR/0102/SC/PW-(FR)/170ARM

A CIP catalogue record for this book
is available from the British Library.

ISBN 0 7534 0706 X

Printed in Hong Kong

Tiger

and the
Temper Tantrum

Vivian French
Rebecca Elgar

KINGFISHER

"Eat up, Tiger,"
said Mother Tiger.

"No," said Tiger.
"I don't like egg.
I want to go to the park
and climb to the top
of the climbing frame."

"We'll go to the park after
we've been to the shop,"
said Mother Tiger.

shop

"Hurry up, Tiger,"
said Mother Tiger.
She wrapped him in
his scarf. "Do you want
to ride in your buggy?"

"No," said Tiger.
"I want to walk.
I want to walk to the park
and climb to the top
of the climbing frame."

In the shop Tiger picked up a big bag of sweeties.

"Put those back, Tiger," said Mother Tiger.

"NO!" said Tiger. "I want sweeties to eat when I go to the park and climb to the top of the climbing frame!"

Mother Tiger put the sweeties back.

Outside the shop Tiger
threw his scarf on the
ground.

"Tiger," said Mother Tiger,
"pick your scarf up."

"No!" Tiger growled.
"I won't! I want to go to the
park! I want to climb to the
top of the climbing frame –
and I want to go NOW!!!"
And he rolled on the ground
waving his paws.

Mother Tiger looked at Tiger.

Mother Tiger roared such a loud roar that Tiger jumped.

"NO," said Mother Tiger. "We're NOT going to the park. We're going HOME. And we're going home THIS MINUTE!"

Tiger stared.

Tiger burst into tears.
Mother Tiger plopped
him into his buggy.
Tiger cried louder.
Mother Tiger walked faster.

"Hello, Tiger," said a voice.

Tiger stopped crying.

"I'm going to the park," said Crocodile.

Tiger sniffed loudly.

"Hi, Tiger!" said Hippo as he skipped by.
"I'm off to the park!"

"WAAAAAAH!!!!
It's not fair!" Tiger wailed.
"Everyone's going to the park except me!"

Mother Tiger stopped.

"Tiger," she said, "maybe Crocodile and Hippo don't have temper tantrums. Maybe Crocodile and Hippo are good little animals . . . and good little animals go to the park!"

Tiger thought very hard.

"Do good little tigers go to the park?" he asked.

"YES!" said Mother Tiger. "Going to the park with good little tigers is FUN!"

"Oh," said Tiger, and he wiped his eyes with his tail. He smoothed his fur with his claws. He smiled a HUGE smile.

"I'm a good tiger now," he said. "A VERY GOOD TIGER!"

And he was –
all the way to the top
of the climbing frame.